Advance
PUBLISHERS

Published by Advance Publishers, L.C.
Maitland, FL 32751 USA
www.advancepublishers.com
Produced by Judy O Productions, Inc.
Designed by SunDried Penguin
© 2006 Disney Enterprises, Inc./Pixar Animation Studios
A Bug's Life
Printed in the United States of America

Princess Atta, who was training to be Queen, was in charge of the annual harvest for the first time. As well as collect food for themselves to last the winter, the ants had to give an offering to the evil grasshopper gang who were expected any minute.

Suddenly the alarm sounded.
The grasshoppers were coming!
All the ants scrambled into the
underground bunker. Flik, a clever
but clumsy inventor-ant, knocked over
the food that the ants had gathered and
it fell into the river far below Ant Island.

Hopper, the chief grasshopper, was really angry that there was no food and said, "We'll be back before winter and we want DOUBLE the amount of grain!"

There was no way the ants could harvest enough grain for the grasshoppers and themselves. Flik knew it was his fault and left Ant Island to find some bigger bugs to help the colony fight the grasshopper gang. He travelled to the city and mistook some circus performers for warrior bugs. The circus bugs thought he was a talent scout and agreed to return to Ant Island with him.

The ants thought Flik had found mighty warriors and Princess Atta thanked the circus bugs for coming to their aid. It was then that the circus bugs realized Flik wasn't a talent scout. They told him they were circus performers and that they had to leave.

As the circus bugs were flying away, Princess Atta's little sister, Dot, followed and was nearly eaten by a hungry sparrow. Francis the ladybug flew up and caught her just in time. But the sparrow kept pecking and Flik and the other bugs saved Dot and Francis in a daring act of bravery. The ants cheered and clapped and the circus bugs were thrilled – success at last. They decided to stay and not mention they weren't warriors to the rest of the colony.

The incident with the sparrow gave Flik a great idea to save the ants from the grasshoppers. Soon the ants and bugs were hard at work building his new invention – a bird made from leaves and twigs. Flik hoped this would frighten Hopper and his gang away.

P.T. Flea, the circus ringmaster, showed up looking for his bugs. Princess Atta saw a poster he had with him and recognized the bugs Flik had brought from the city. She was very upset Flik had lied and said they were warriors, when they were just circus performers. She told Flik and the bugs to leave Ant Island and never come back.

When Hopper and his gang arrived to collect the grain, they were furious that there wasn't enough. They raided the ants' storeroom of winter food and made a plan to make the ants work as slaves and then squish the Queen. Dot overheard the plan and flew off to find Flik and the circus bugs.

Flik and his new pals came up with a plan of their own. The circus bugs entertained Hopper and his gang while Flik and Dot climbed inside the fake bird and launched it into the air. Hopper and his gang fled in terror – but P.T. Flea was upset the bird was ruining the circus performance and set fire to it.

Flik's bird crash-landed and Hopper realized he'd been tricked! But, this time, Princess Atta stood up to Hopper with thousands of ants behind her, united by courage. Hopper grabbed Flik and tried to escape, but Princess Atta raced to Flik's rescue and they flew across the river to where the hungry sparrow lived. Hopper thought it was another trick bird and the sparrow gobbled him up!

When spring arrived, the circus bugs left to perform in the city. Princess Atta was now the Queen and she named Flik honorary Ant Island inventor. He was living proof that one little ant can make a difference.

The End